RUSS THOMPSON

CW00864099

PLACE
TO
HIDE

**High-Interest
Press**

Editing by Laura Perkins. Series
concept by Pam Sheppard. Cover by
Shayne at Wicked Good Book Covers.
Print text set in Open Dyslexic
Mono. File HP001.32C.2021.03.23.
Website www.highinterestpress.com.

Lexile measure HL420L.

For Betty-Jean,
our kids,
and grandkids.

CONTENTS

1 NOW THEY KNOW

ENGLISH. I know I'm not a good reader. But I know how to cover it up.

I smile at the teachers, keep my hand down, print neatly, and nod when they explain things.

I'm in the tenth grade now, so I've been doing it for a long time.

The teacher comes to the front of the classroom. We have a sub again.

She's old, kind of hunched over, with a tired look on her face.

"My name is Ms. Gulliver," she

says. "You will pay attention, do your work, and raise your hand to speak. If there's a problem, you will get detention. I will also call your parents."

I know how to act in class, so this doesn't bother me.

"Another thing I want you to know, is that I do not call on volunteers," she says. "I will call on you at random from the roll book. You will have to be ready at all times."

Now, I'm worried.

She hands out some papers.

"This is a news article from the *Conroy Courier*," she says. "Please begin reading. When you finish, write one paragraph to explain what it's about."

A picture in the article shows an

old man standing next to a cop car.
I can only read some of the words.

I pick out some sentences and
begin copying. I don't understand
what the article is about. But at
least my printing is neat.

Ten minutes pass.

"Time's up," Ms. Gulliver says.
"Please read your paragraph when I
call on you."

She looks in the roll book. I
feel nervous.

"Jessie Soto," she says. "Please
begin."

I'm glad she didn't call on me.
He reads his paragraph smoothly.

Ms. Gulliver looks in the roll
book again. I hunch down in my seat.
I don't want her to call on me.

"Owen Daniels," she says. "Your
turn."

I pretend not to hear. Maybe she'll call on somebody else.

"Owen Daniels," Ms. Gulliver says. "Please begin."

Everybody looks at me. I'm probably turning red.

I don't know all the words. But I have to read.

"Conroy Police are looking for three ar... armed sus... suspects in connect... connection... with a home inva... invasion... robbery on Sunday. The vic... victim, a 62-year-old man, was stuck... struck... in the head with a handgun and received mul... multiply... lacer... lacerations. Cash and jewels were taken from the resi... residence."

Now they know. There's no place to hide. I just showed everyone how dumb I am.

2   DON'T THINK

TUESDAY MORNING. Katie and I walk through the front gate of Edison High School.

We get to the twelfth-grade lockers.

She turns and hurries off quickly, like she doesn't want to be seen with me.

She's my sister, and I embarrass her. I've known it for a while.

She's one of the smart ones. I'm one of the dumb ones.

MATH. Mr. Braden stands at the door when I get there.

He smiles at the smart students. But he never smiles at me.

I take my seat and get ready to be confused.

"Today we're starting word problems," Mr. Braden says. "That's what math is. It's about using numbers to do things in real life."

He calls on a girl to read the problem on the board. I read along with her. But I can't understand it.

This is my second time taking algebra. I can do the numbers. But I can't do the words.

It's as bad this year as it was last year.

LUNCH. I go to the food court, get my lunch, and sit in the back with

Alex and Fernando.

"We had a sub again in English today," Alex says. "Three guys in there were ditching from other classes."

"What happened?" I ask.

"When the sub took attendance, she made us say our ID numbers. The guys who were ditching got caught."

"Who was the sub?" Fernando asks.

"Ms. Gulliver," Alex says. "The one who's real old."

The fear I felt yesterday comes back to me. What if she calls on me again?

ENGLISH. Ms. Gulliver stands at the door with a paperback book in her hand.

I don't want her to notice me. I look down and try to sneak past her.

13

"Owen," she says. "I thought you might like this book. It's about a family that gets caught in a hurricane."

I've never had a teacher give me a book before. I go to my desk and look through the pages.

The title is *I Survived Hurricane Katrina.* The cover shows a kid caught in a flood.

Most of the words seem okay. Maybe it's a book I can read.

Ms. Gulliver comes to the front of the classroom.

"The principal talked to me at lunch," she says. "Ms. Knox had a baby boy this morning."

Some of the students start clapping. Then everybody claps.

"I don't know how long she'll be gone," Ms. Gulliver says. "But I

might be here for the rest of the
school year."

The room gets quiet.

I don't want her for my teacher,
even if she did give me a book.

Sooner or later, she's going to
call on me again.

AFTERNOON. I go downstairs to Alex's
apartment. He's ready when I knock
on the door.

We get on our skateboards and
ride to the Taco Slab.

It used to be a fast-food place
called Taco Time. But it burned down
one night. Now, it's just a big slab
of concrete next to Mike's Market.

I do some low Ollies and rail
stands. Alex mostly does kickflips.

Mr. Mike comes out of the market
with his coffee cup.

He used to be a football player, and he's huge. The old chair he sits on looks like it could break any minute.

"You guys are doing better on those tricks," he says. "But what's going on with your grades?"

"They come out tonight on School View," Alex says.

"Good," Mr. Mike says. "I want to see them tomorrow."

Ever since we were little, Mr. Mike has been giving us free stuff for our grades.

I don't think I'll be getting anything this time.

3   NEVER

TUESDAY AFTERNOON. Living room. I sit on the couch, which is also my bed.

Katie still isn't home from volleyball practice. I turn on the TV and start *Gunner*.

My game name is Sarge. I have big arms that tear the sleeves of my army uniform.

I run across a field with my machine gun and hide behind a blown-up troop carrier.

A helicopter flies toward me, its machine guns blasting.

I jump to the side and keep running. Three enemies shoot at me.

I hit the ground and crawl into a bomb crater.

They're coming for me. I raise my gun and fire.

A key turns in the door lock. I turn off the TV and pick up the book Ms. Gulliver gave me.

Katie steps in. I didn't think she would be home so soon.

"Owen," she says. "I could hear your game from outside. Mom told you, no video games until you finish your homework."

"I know what she said. Don't worry about it."

"You're the one who should be

worrying. That's why you're messing up in school."

Sometimes I can't stand her. I'm glad when she leaves the room.

FIVE-THIRTY. I stand at the stove, frying chicken. Katie opens a box of noodles and puts on a pan of water to boil.

When it comes to cooking, I'm twenty times better than her.

"I think I might get all A's on my report card again," she says.

I sprinkle pepper on the chicken. "Good for you."

She wants me to tell her what I'm getting. But it's none of her business.

I'm tired of Katie and her straight A's.

Her picture is on the wall at

Edison for being on the honor roll.

I have to look at it every day.

AFTER DINNER. I sit at the kitchen table and open the laptop.

The hinge is broken, so I have to be careful with it.

I get on School View and go to the screen for tenth graders.

In math, we have three word-problems. The first one is like the one we had in class today.

I read the words. But I can't understand it.

It's the same for the other two. I copy the problems, show some work, and write down some answers.

I know they're wrong. But the printing is neat. It should be good enough for a checkmark.

Next, I go to the website for

science. We have to read four pages and answer the questions.

I don't understand any of it, so I copy some sentences and add a few words of my own.

In history, I do the same. I also copy for English.

I don't know what I did. But at least it's done.

EIGHT O'CLOCK. I click on School View and put in my password. The grade screen comes on.

In art, my grade is a B. In PE, I have a B. But I have NoPasses in math, science, history, and English.

Four NoPasses. These are the worst grades I've ever had.

ELEVEN O'CLOCK. I unfold the couch, get under the blankets, and turn out the light.

Mom's going to be mad when she gets home and sees my grades.

The front door opens. I pretend to sleep while Mom comes inside.

She steps past my bed into the kitchen.

I hear typing on the laptop. She's probably looking at Katie's grades.

I hear more typing. She's probably looking at my grades.

I hate school.

4 DON'T LIKE

THURSDAY MORNING. SCIENCE. The warm-up assignment is on the board.

Read page 84. Write three sentences about the main idea.

I open my book. The page has two pictures.

The first one shows an old guy with white hair, Thomas Edison.

The second picture shows a kid turning a crank on a device with wires connected to a lightbulb.

I copy one sentence from the beginning of the page, one from the middle, and one from the end.

"Raise your hands," Ms. Acosta says. "Who would like to read?"

I'm glad she only calls on volunteers. A girl named Esmeralda raises her hand. I listen as she reads her sentences.

"Thomas Edison was a genius who built thousands of inventions," she says. "One of them was the electric lightbulb. He failed countless times until it finally worked."

She reads perfectly, just like I wish I could.

"Go back to the page and look at the picture of the device with the crank on it," Ms. Acosta says. "What is it?"

"It's an electric generator,"

Esmeralda says.

"That's right," Ms. Acosta says. "And it's a good example of something you could build for the science fair. I hope you all think about making a project."

I know she's not talking to me.

I think I could build the generator. But I could never write the report.

ENGLISH. Ms. Gulliver comes to the front of the classroom.

"This is a test of your reading skills," she says. "Read the passage carefully. Answer the questions in your own words."

I look at the words. There are too many big ones.

I copy some sentences for my answers. That's the best I can do.

The next part of class is silent reading. I take out my book, *I Survived Hurricane Katrina.*

I'm still on the first chapter. I don't want anyone to see how easy it is, so I shield it with my arms.

Ms. Gulliver kneels next to my desk and whispers to me. "I need to talk to you for a minute after class. Wait here when the bell rings."

I wonder what she wants to talk about. Nothing she says is going to help.

Then it happens. The dream comes back.

I stand outside a school bus. The door is locked. I can't get on. The other students point and laugh at me. The bus drives away. I run to

*catch it. But I can't run fast
enough.*

AFTER CLASS. Everybody else leaves
the classroom.

I don't want to talk to Ms.
Gulliver, but I have to.

She comes over and sits in the
desk next to me.

"Owen, how much do you read now?"
she asks.

"Not much," I say.

"Have you ever read a whole
book?"

"I've read parts of books. But
not a whole one."

"You're behind in your reading,"
she says. "But you can catch up if
you read more. Tell your mom I'm
going to call her tonight. It's
important."

I nod. But reading is a lost cause for me.

EVENING. It's Mom's night off, so we're making dinner together.

I cut up some tomatoes for a salad.

"Owen, I got a call from Ms. Gulliver," Mom says. "We had a long talk."

I get a bad feeling. I didn't want Mom to know about my reading.

"She told me you have to read more," Mom says. "She also said you have to slow down and learn the new words when you read, not skip over them."

"We worked out a plan to help you improve your reading," Mom says. "You will read every night for thirty minutes in a book of your choice. You will also keep a list of all the new words you find."

"I'm going to get you a paperback dictionary, so you can look up the words. Each morning after breakfast, I will look at your word list and have you read to me. Each night after dinner, you will also read to Katie."

This is too much. It's not going to work.

Ms. Gulliver is wrong.

Mom is wrong.

And I won't read to Katie.

5 MAYBE

FRIDAY EVENING. I sit at the top of
the stairs outside our apartment.

I finished my thirty minutes of
reading. I also read to Katie.

It wasn't as bad as I thought it
would be.

Uncle Ray pulls up in his tow
truck. I go down the stairs and
climb into the cab.

I've never gone out with him
before. I hope it goes okay.

"Put on the reflector vest,"
Uncle Ray says. "I don't want you

getting run over. Also, whatever I say, you have to do it right away. No questions."

I like the way he talks to me, not like I'm a little kid. I put on the vest and buckle my seatbelt.

He pulls into traffic. I wonder what's going to happen tonight.

THIRTY MINUTES LATER. We're on our way to a car with a flat tire.

I see an orange hammer with a pointed head in the door pocket.

"What's this for?" I ask.

"It's for breaking car windows in an emergency," Uncle Ray says. "A regular hammer doesn't work because the glass in cars is so hard."

We stop at a red light. I wonder why Uncle Ray has been so quiet tonight.

"Owen, we need to talk," he says. "Your mom told me about your grades."

I was afraid of this. Now I know why he's been so quiet.

"She's worried," Uncle Ray says. "She's scared you're going to turn out like your dad."

It hurts to hear him say that. My dad is in prison back in Ohio.

I've never even seen him.

SEVEN O'CLOCK. A call comes over the radio. There's a traffic accident on Hester Boulevard.

Uncle Ray steps on the gas. I feel my heart pound.

"When we get there, stay in the truck," he says. "Don't do anything unless I tell you."

Five minutes later, we pull up to

the crash.

The first car is a silver SUV with its front torn up. Uncle Ray runs to it. He signals to me that the driver is okay.

The second car is a white Honda with its side smashed in. The man inside has blood running down his face. Uncle Ray stays with him.

A fire truck, paramedics, and a police car roll up.

The paramedics put the man on a gurney and take him away.

Uncle Ray comes back to the tow truck.

"Is he going to be okay?" I ask.

"He was cut up," Uncle Ray says. "But I don't think there was anything major."

He gives me the okay to get out of the tow truck.

We sweep up the broken glass together. I feel good, like I'm doing a job.

But when we hook up the Honda to the tow truck, I see blood on the front seat.

I wish I wasn't there.

GOLDEN GRILL. I feel better now. Uncle Ray and I sit next to the front window. Edison High School is across the street.

They call our number. We get our burgers and come back to the table.

"What was it like when you went to Edison?" I ask.

"I played around and failed a lot of classes", Uncle Ray says. "It was fifteen years ago. I barely made it through."

It surprises me to hear him say

that. I never knew he had trouble in school.

"Luckily, I came out of it," he says. "I had a teacher who helped me. Her name was Ms. Gulliver. She gave me books to read."

"That's who I have. She gave me a book about a kid in a hurricane."

"Make sure you listen to her," Uncle Ray says. "Ms. Gulliver is the reason why I graduated."

Maybe she won't be so bad.

6 WON'T BE EASY

SATURDAY MORNING. I open to Chapter
Three in *I Survived Hurricane
Katrina*. I also take out my
paperback dictionary.

I begin reading, look up the new
words, and write them on my word
list. Thirty minutes later, I'm
done.

It's a lot of time to spend on
reading. I hope it works.

LATER. Time for a break. I go down
the back stairs to the alley and

open the garage.

It always feels good to walk inside. I have my workbench. I have my tools. It's a place where I can fix and make things.

I'm rebuilding a tricycle for my cousin, Leo.

It has a lot of rust on it. And the wheels don't turn.

First, I take it apart and put the pieces in a cardboard box.

Next, I wash the parts in a bucket of laundry soap. I clean off the rust with steel wool, rinse the parts, and put them on a towel to dry.

Sanding the frame is next. I use wet-dry sandpaper and work carefully to get it smooth.

I wash the frame again, rinse it in clear water, and dry it.

The last step for today is painting. I hang the frame from one of the rafters and spray it with gray primer.

The final coat, bright yellow, will go on tomorrow.

It will be fun to see Leo's face when he gets his new tricycle.

LATER. I put my tools away. The garage is clean now.

Alex walks in. "Owen, you ready to lift?"

I have a steel weight bar and a hundred pounds of iron plates that Uncle Ray got for me at a garage sale.

Alex and I have been lifting for three weeks.

We start with curls and shoulder presses. Then we do push-ups, lunges, squats, and calf raises.

"You know what else we can do?"
Alex asks.

"What?"

"We can do pull-ups on the PE
yard when we get to school in the
morning."

"Good idea," I say. "It should
make a big difference over time."

I look at my arms. I feel like
I'm getting stronger now.

It makes me feel good about
myself.

AFTERNOON. I get on my skateboard
and ride to Price Mart. I need a can
of yellow spray paint for Leo's
tricycle.

Mom is working today. I wonder if
I'll see her.

I go inside, find the paint I

need, and turn to go.

An old man stops me. He's carrying a can of house paint.

"Could you look at this label for me?" he asks. "I left my glasses at home. Is this exterior paint, or interior?"

I look at the label. But there are too many words I don't know.

"Sorry," I say. "I don't have my glasses, either."

I look over his shoulder. Mom watches us. I hope she didn't hear what I said.

The man turns and shows Mom the label. I hurry to leave.

I don't want her to say anything to me.

LATE AFTERNOON. I sit at the kitchen table, reading my *I Survived* book and writing on my word list.

A key turns in the front door. Mom comes in and sits at the kitchen table across from me.

"I saw what happened when that man asked you to read the paint can," Mom says. "How come you told him you wore glasses?"

"I don't know."

"Is it because you didn't know the words?"

"I guess so."

"That's why you have to read every day," she says. "It will take time. But if you read every day for thirty minutes and keep your word list, each day you will get better."

She makes it sound easy. But it's not.

7 PROVE I'M NOT

MONDAY MORNING. SCIENCE. Ms. Acosta points to the board.

We have to tell what we remember from last week about Thomas Edison. I begin writing.

Owen Daniels
Science 10

Thomas Edson

Thomas Edson was a famuss inventer who invent the lightbub. He was deaff but still made invenshins.

Edson high school is nammed after him. He is one of the most famuss inventers of all time.

I know I have a lot of mistakes. But it's the best I can do.

Ms. Acosta comes to the front of the classroom.

"You're going to complete group projects on famous inventors this week," she says. "Each of you will write a one-page report as part of your group work."

She puts me onto a team with Brooks and Esmeralda.

Brooks is okay. But Esmeralda is stuck up. I can tell by the look on her face that she doesn't want me in the group.

"Let's do our project on Thomas

Edison," Esmeralda says. "I'll take his early life."

"I'll do his inventions," Brooks says.

That leaves me with his career. I have to write a whole page.

AFTERNOON. I sit at the kitchen table. The draft of my science report is due tomorrow.

I open the laptop and type Thomas Edison into the browser.

The websites are no good. They have too many words I don't know.

But one of the sites has a video. It's a silent movie from the 1920's.

The film shows Thomas Edison going to work at a factory where they make his inventions.

During the movie, words come on the screen to tell what's happening.

Everything is old because it happened a hundred years ago.

I don't know what to write for my report. Then, I get an idea.

If I copy the words that come on the screen, that can be my report.

Owen Daniels
Science 10

Thomas Edison

Thomas Edison's inventions have been beneficial to millions of people.

He lives close to the laboratory he established in West Orange, New Jersey.

He arrives to work early, punches a time clock, and works from a desk in the middle of the laboratory.

His assistants bring important

matters to him for his decisions.

They must speak into his ear because he is deaf.

His factory builds incandescent lightbulbs. Women operate the machines that place tungsten wires inside the bulbs.

Mr. Edison considers himself a working man. At the end of the day, he punches out at the time clock and rides home in his flivver.

I know I shouldn't copy. But I think I can get away with it.

It has a lot of big words I don't know. I take out my dictionary and begin looking them up.

I'll be reading the report to Brooks and Esmeralda tomorrow. I have to know the words perfectly.

8 GLAD

TUESDAY MORNING. SCIENCE. Ms. Acosta comes to the front of the classroom.

"Sit in your groups," she says. "Read your reports to each other and discuss them. You will present your projects tomorrow."

Brooks and Esmeralda read their reports. They sound perfect. I don't know how they do it.

Next, it's my turn. I'm nervous. But I read my report without any mistakes. Brooks and Esmeralda look surprised.

"Owen, I can tell you copied," Esmeralda says. "Those are not your own words. I bet you don't even know what they mean."

"Ask me," I say.

"What's a flivver?" she asks.

"It's an old car."

"What does beneficial mean?"

"It means helpful."

"What does established mean?"

"It means started."

"I don't care," she says. "I still know you copied. And you're not going to fool Ms. Acosta."

If Ms. Acosta finds out I copied, it will be a NoPass.

But Brooks doesn't say anything. Maybe it will be okay.

AFTER SCHOOL. It feels good to be outside. Alex and I skate to the

Taco Slab.

Mr. Mike comes out of the market and sits in his usual spot.

I do a kickflip and fall on my side. I get up and try again. This time, I make it.

Mr. Mike sips his coffee.

"You guys remind me of my football days," he says. "You fall down. But you get up and keep going. That's a good way to be."

That's what I like about Mr. Mike. He makes me feel good about myself.

ELEVEN O'CLOCK. I sit at the kitchen table. It's hard to stay awake. I wish I could go to bed.

I read my science report again to make sure I know all the words. I can't make any mistakes when I read

49

it to the class tomorrow.

I'm tired. I put my head down to rest for a minute.

SOMEONE SHAKES MY SHOULDER. I open my eyes. It's Mom.

"You fell asleep," she says.

I sit up and wipe my eyes.

"What are you working on?" she asks. "You drooled all over it."

I look down. The center of my paper is wet. The ink is smeared.

"It's my science report," I say. "I have to read it to the class tomorrow."

"Let me hear it," she says.

I read the words perfectly. I know she's going to say she's proud of me.

But instead, she frowns.

"You are not going to turn this

in," she says. "I can tell that you copied. It doesn't sound like you. I'm going to sit here while you write it in your own words."

Mom sits with me and drinks coffee while I work. If I spell a word wrong, she makes me look it up and write it five times.

It takes forever. When I finish, it's almost one o'clock in the morning.

"Good job," Mom says. "This time, I'm proud of you."

All I want now, is to sleep.

9 LIKE IT NOW

WEDNESDAY MORNING. I sit at the kitchen table and pour a bowl of cereal.

"Why are you yawning?" Katie asks.

"I had to finish a report for science."

Mom comes into the kitchen. She's yawning too.

"Owen," she says. "Good job again."

Katie looks at us like she's trying to figure things out.

"Was school ever hard for you?" Katie asks Mom.

"I got good grades," Mom says. "But I went to work right after high school instead of going to college. I'm paying for it now."

"What do you mean?"

"Not going to college is holding me back at my job."

"But you're a supervisor."

"That's right," Mom says. "But I might be a manager now if I had gone to college."

SCIENCE. This is it. I try not to be nervous.

Ms. Acosta stands at the front of the classroom. "When I call your group, come up and begin reading."

She walks to the back and sits in the empty desk next to me.

The first group begins. Their project is about Alexander Graham Bell, the guy who invented the telephone.

The first two reports are good. But the third report, by Perla, has a lot of big words she would never use.

"What is an innovator?" Ms. Acosta asks her.

"A famous person."

"What does an innovator do?"

"Make famous things."

"What is an innovation?"

"A thing that is famous."

I watch Ms. Acosta's hand. She writes a NoPass on the grade sheet.

I'm glad Mom helped me last night.

Our group is next. We walk to the front. I try not to be nervous.

Ms. Acosta smiles as Brooks and Esmeralda read their reports.

"Owen, your turn," Ms. Acosta says.

My hands shake. I take a breath and begin reading. It seems like it takes forever.

Ms. Acosta smiles when I finish.

"Good report," Esmeralda whispers to me.

It's a shock. I can't believe she said something nice to me.

I go back to my seat. Ms. Acosta writes on her grade sheet. She gives me a B.

Another shock. I've never gotten a B on anything in science before.

ENGLISH. Ms. Gulliver comes to the front of the classroom.

"Get out your books," she says.

"The first fifteen minutes will be sustained silent reading."

I'm on Chapter Five of *I Survived Hurricane Katrina*.

I open the book. Ms. Gulliver comes over and kneels next to me.

"How is it?" she asks.

"It's starting to get easier. I understand more of the words now."

"How's your word list?"

I open it and show her. I also show her the dictionary Mom bought for me.

"You're on the right track," Ms. Gulliver says. "Keep doing what you're doing."

"But it's slow."

"That's okay," she says. "It's going to take time. But if you keep reading, you'll get there."

She gets up. I go back to my

reading.

I come to a word I don't know,
look it up, and put it on my word
list.

I'm going to keep trying.

AFTER DINNER. I sit at the kitchen
table with my *I Survived* book. Katie
sits next to me.

I read to her and show her my
word list. It's seven pages long.

"Good job," Katie says. "You're
getting better."

I never thought I would want
Katie to help me with my reading.

But I like it now.

10 NOT GOING

THURSDAY MORNING. The bell rings. I leave math and step into the hallway.

Nancy and Natalie from science walk in front of me. They don't know I'm behind them.

"Could you believe the report that Owen read yesterday?" Nancy asks. "It was actually good."

"There's no way it was his," Natalie says. "I've known him since third grade. He's too stupid to write anything like that."

I move to the side and stop. It's like a slap in the face.

ENGLISH. It's been bothering me all day. I can't stop thinking about what Nancy and Natalie said about me.

Ms. Gulliver comes to the front of the classroom. I think she's going to give one of her speeches.

"When I was in school, I had problems with reading," she says. "One time I heard some students say I was dumb."

I can't believe she's saying this. She seems so smart.

"It hurt," Ms. Gulliver says. "But I had a teacher who helped me. She gave me some easy books, some books I could read."

"I started reading," Ms. Gulliver

says. "The more I read, the smarter I got. After a while, I was getting B's and C's in my classes instead of D's."

"Smart is not something you are," she says. "Smart is something you make yourself. And you can all make yourself smarter by working hard."

I look at Nancy and Natalie. I'm going to prove them wrong.

I don't know how long it will take.

But I'm going to work hard.

And I'm not going to stop.

11   COP WAS RIGHT

FRIDAY NIGHT. I sit outside on the steps, waiting for Uncle Ray. I'll be glad when he gets here.

He pulls up in the tow truck. I jump in and put on my safety vest.

I see the window hammer in the door pocket. I wonder if it works.

"Owen, how was school this week?" Uncle Ray asks.

"I got a B on a science report. I also started reading for thirty minutes a night and keeping a word list."

"Did you say hi to Ms. Gulliver for me?"

"I did. She smiled when I told her about you. She wants you to stop by."

A radio call comes in. "11-80, 10-79, 12-86. Hester and Rayburn."

Uncle Ray makes a U-turn and steps on the gas.

"Traffic accident," he says. "Four blocks from here. Don't get out of this truck for any reason."

I sit up straight. It sounds bad.

HESTER AND RAYBURN. A pickup truck has smashed into the back of a van.

The front of the truck burns. The van fills with smoke.

There's a lady inside the van. She can't get out.

People on the curb stand and

watch.

Uncle Ray runs to the van, opens the front door, and cuts the seatbelt with his knife.

He pulls the lady free and helps her get away from the van.

"My kids!" she screams." They're in the back seat!"

Uncle Ray runs to the passenger door and pulls on the handle. It won't open.

Flames spread inside the van. The kids scream. They can't get out.

A police car rolls up with its red lights flashing.

A cop jumps out and tries to smash the side window with his flashlight.

It doesn't break.

Uncle Ray told me to stay in the truck. I can't do it.

I grab the window hammer, run to the van, and break the side window.

Uncle Ray reaches inside and pulls the first kid out. The cop grabs the second kid.

Flames fill the van.

The mom kneels and pulls her kids to her.

They're okay.

A fire truck pulls up. The firemen jump out and spray water on the van.

The police officer walks over to me. "Do you know what you did?"

"I broke the window."

"That's not what I'm talking about. You saved those kids' lives."

He shakes my hand and looks me in the eye. "You're a hero."

My body goes limp. Those kids almost died.

LATER. Uncle Ray and I are back at the tow yard, washing the truck.

"I'm glad you didn't listen to me when I told you to stay in the truck," he says.

I turn on the hose nozzle and rinse off the suds.

"I keep seeing it in my mind and hearing those kids scream. I thought they were going to die."

"You didn't just stand around and watch, like the rest of those people," Uncle Ray says. "You came forward and did something."

Tears come to my eyes. I wipe them with my sleeve.

Uncle Ray puts his arm around me. "That cop was right. You really are a hero."

12 MAYBE I CAN

SATURDAY MORNING. We finish breakfast. Mom leaves for work.

I go downstairs and knock on Alex's door.

We throw down our boards and skate to the Taco Slab.

Mr. Mike comes out and sits in his chair with his coffee cup.

"Good to see you guys," he says.

Alex does a pop-shove-it. I try a kickflip but miss.

Mr. Mike goes back into his market.

He comes out with two sodas, two hot dogs, and a bag of some other stuff.

He gives us the dogs. We begin eating.

He gives me the bag and shakes my hand.

"Owen, this is for your mom," he says. "It's for what you did to save those kids."

I open the bag. It has bread, Spam, milk, and Raisin Bran.

"How did you know about the kids?" I ask.

"I hear everything that goes on around here. You did a brave thing last night."

A few minutes later, we're skating home.

"You're a hero now," Alex says. "You even got Spam."

MIDMORNING. Alex and I lift weights in the garage. We finish curls and start shoulder presses.

"When you ran to that van, weren't you scared that it was going to blow up?" Alex asks.

"Everything was happening so fast. All I knew, was that those kids were going to die."

I see the van burning in my head. I hear their mom screaming.

I wish it would quit coming back to me.

ONE O'CLOCK. Alex and I ride our skateboards to the library. Mom said I have to go every Saturday now.

We get there and look through the shelves. I find a book on Thomas Edison.

It has a picture on the front

that shows him with a lightbulb.

It's a little-kid book. But I can read most of the words, so I keep it.

It also has pictures of his inventions. I think about the generator we saw in our science book.

I wonder if I could build it.

AFTERNOON. I sit on the couch to read Chapter Eight in *I Survived Hurricane Katrina*.

The hurricane winds are blowing now. Water floods the house.

The family goes to the second floor. The water rises higher.

They go to the attic. The water keeps coming. The family is trapped.

How will they get out?

I read Chapter Nine. After that,

Chapter Ten. Two hours later, I'm done.

Katie comes into the living room. "How is your book?"

"I just finished it."

"Let's celebrate," she says. "I have some money. We can go to Burger House."

I never thought a book could be exciting.

I never thought I would finish one.

And I never thought Katie would want to celebrate with me.

AFTER DINNER. I open up my book about Thomas Edison.

The first part tells about him as a kid.

A teacher told Edison's mom that he was stupid and would never learn.

His mom told the teacher she was wrong and began teaching Thomas at home.

Ms. Gulliver keeps saying that we can all be successful, and that we make ourselves smart.

That's what Thomas Edison did. Maybe I can, too.

13 KEEP READING

MONDAY MORNING. Alex and I walk to school. I feel myself moving faster than normal.

"How come you're in such a hurry?" Alex asks.

"I don't know."

What's really happening, is that I'm excited about getting to school.

If Mr. Mike heard about the van crash, everybody at school will also know about it.

I'll be a hero.

We reach school and go through

the front gate.

This is it. I'm famous now. I'm ready for the high-fives.

But nothing happens.

Everybody walks by me like they always do.

I'm still a nobody.

SCIENCE. The bell rings to end class. I accidentally knock my backpack off the desk.

My book on Thomas Edison falls out. I reach down. But Nancy grabs it first.

"Nice book," she says. "I think I read it in third grade."

She gives it to Natalie, who waves it in the air for everybody to see.

I feel like a fool.

LUNCH. I stand in line at the food court. Two guys stand ahead of me. I don't know them.

"Did you hear about the car crash and the van that caught on fire?" the first one asks.

"Yeah. I heard some kids almost burned to death."

"Guess who helped save them?"

"Who?"

"Some guy named Owen. He almost got blown up."

"I wonder what he looks like."

"I don't know. But whoever he is, what he did was no joke."

I feel good inside.

ENGLISH. We're writing essays on a current event from the newspaper.

Ms. Gulliver walks around the room and stops at my desk. I pull out my book report on *I Survived Hurricane Katrina.*

"This is for you," I say. "It was a good book."

"Nice job. You finished it faster than I thought you would."

"I was reading one chapter a day. Then it got really good. I finished the whole thing on Saturday."

"That's what happens when you start reading," Ms. Gulliver says.

I open my backpack and take out my Edison book. I don't try to hide the cover from the other students.

"I'm reading this one now," I say.

"Very good," she says. "You're doing what I talked about. You're making yourself smart."

I'm still mad about what Nancy and Natalie did. But I don't care what they think anymore.

And I don't care what the others think.

I'm going to keep reading.

I'll choose whatever I want.

I'm going to read every night.

I'm going to read on the weekends.

I'm going to read every book I can.

14   SMART ONES

MONDAY MORNING. Six months later. I get to school with Alex.

We go straight to the PE yard and the pull-up bars. Alex does twelve pull-ups. I do ten.

I look at my arms. They're a lot stronger now.

"How's your science project?" Alex asks.

"I can't get the generator to work."

"What's wrong with it?"

"I don't know. I did everything

right. But the lightbulb doesn't come on."

We leave the PE yard. The science fair is this Wednesday. There isn't much time.

SCIENCE. Ms. Acosta comes to the front of the classroom.

"Raise your hand," she says. "How many of you are still doing a project for the science fair?"

Five people raise their hands. Brooks is one of them.

I raise mine last. I don't like the other kids looking at me.

"If you need to print your report, I'll be here after school," Ms. Acosta says. "If it isn't typed, I will take points off."

We have a printer at home, so I don't have to worry.

I just have to get my generator to work.

ENGLISH. Ms. Gulliver comes to the front of the classroom.

"How many of you would like to go to college someday?"

I'm not sure. But I raise my hand like everybody else.

"Remember," she says. "It's not just about college. It's about higher education. You can go to a university. You can also go to a community college or trade school."

Things have changed for me in the last six months. I read every night for at least thirty minutes, sometimes more. I've finished thirty-two books this year.

I've also been working hard in my classes. My grades are all B's and

C's now.

Maybe I can get to be one of the smart ones.

15 WRONG

MONDAY AFTERNOON. I'm in the garage, working on my generator. I still can't get it to work.

I carry it upstairs to the kitchen, get on YouTube, and check the directions again.

The video shows a guy turning the crank on a generator made with magnets and wires. A tiny lightbulb comes on when he turns the crank.

Mine is just like it. What did I do wrong?

Katie comes into the kitchen.

"Owen, how's the generator?"

"It won't work. I built it exactly like the video. But the lightbulb won't come on."

Katie looks at the project and plays the video.

"I hate to say it," she says. "But I don't think you wound enough wire on the generator coils. And what about your magnets? Are they strong enough?"

"What do you mean?"

"How much do you know about generators?"

"I thought I could just follow the video."

"That's the problem," she says. "You need to know what you're doing. Did you check the comments on the website?"

"What do you mean?"

She scrolls down and goes to the comments.

"Look here," she says. "Most of the comments say it doesn't work. You have to find a video that's for real, not some stupid thing that somebody put on YouTube to get hits and make money."

I watch as she types *Science Project Generator* into the search box.

She comes to a video that shows a generator made from wire wrapped around a little cardboard box. A crank turns magnets inside the box. A light comes on when the crank is turned.

The comments say it works. The project also has several pages of plans that explain how to build it and why it works.

"This project is real, isn't it?" I ask.

"Yep. This is the one you should have built."

I watch the video again. The man who builds the generator is an electrical engineer.

He goes step-by-step, showing exactly what to do. He also explains why it works.

I print out the plans and read everything carefully.

Katie comes back to the kitchen.

"I know how to build it," I say. "But I only have seven dollars to buy the parts."

"That's all right," Katie says. "I can lend you the rest."

CABOT BOULEVARD. I push hard and go as fast as I can on my skateboard.

Time is running out.

The electronics store is two miles away. It closes at six.

Fifteen minutes later, I go in the front door.

The man at the counter is an old guy with a dirty shirt. I give him my list of parts.

"Are you the one who called?" he asks.

"That's me."

"Are you building a generator?"

"How did you know?"

"My grandson built one. He used the same parts you're getting. It works great."

He gets me 30-gauge wire, four magnets, and a 1.5-volt tiny lightbulb.

I'll be able to make the generator now.

I run out the door and skate home
as fast as I can.

KITCHEN. I set up the laptop, get on
YouTube, and look at the video
again. I follow the instructions
carefully.

The last step is to connect the
wires to the lightbulb.

I turn the crank. The bulb
doesn't light. I crank it again.
Nothing. I crank again as fast as I
can. Nothing.

Katie comes in.

"Can you tell what's wrong?" I
ask her.

She looks at the generator and
checks the wires. She also reads the
directions on the website.

"Everything looks good," she
says. "I can't tell what the problem

is."

The clock is ticking. I have to figure it out.

I read the directions again and again.

I check more websites. I read everything I can find about how to generate electricity.

What did I do wrong?

16   LOOKS BAD

TUESDAY MORNING. This is it. I have to finish my science project today.

If I don't, everybody will think I'm stupid.

I fold up the couch, get dressed, and go to the kitchen for breakfast.

I look at the stove and think. It cooks with electricity. I wonder how many volts it uses.

Then it hits me. My project. I didn't check the voltage on the lightbulb.

I look in the trashcan for the

package of the bulb I bought.

It says 3.6 volts. That's too high. The bulb was supposed to be 1.5 volts.

Now I know what happened. There's nothing wrong with the generator.

The voltage on the lightbulb is wrong.

I can get the right bulb after school. But I'm running out of time.

The science fair is tomorrow.

AFTER SCHOOL. I skate as fast as I can to the electronics store.

I'm out of breath when I get there. I tell the man what happened.

He goes to the back and comes out with the correct bulb.

"Try this," he says.

I hook it up to the generator and turn the crank. The light comes on.

The man tries it too. It works every time.

"I'm giving you two extra bulbs," he says. "You might need some spares for the science fair."

I thank him, run out the door, and skate home as fast as I can.

AFTER DINNER. I begin typing the report into the laptop. My project is going to be perfect.

Katie comes into the kitchen. "Do you know that you're doing the same thing Thomas Edison did?"

"What's that?"

"When his experiments failed, he just kept trying. That's what you've been doing."

It's nice of her to say that. After all this work, I'm going to have a good project.

TEN O'CLOCK. I finish typing. It feels great to be almost done.

I click on the touchpad to print my report. Nothing comes out of the printer.

I click again. Nothing.

I try once more. Still nothing.

The printer is out of ink.

I pound my fist on the table. I can't believe this is happening.

But I'm not going to quit.

I get a pen and begin copying the report by hand.

ELEVEN O'CLOCK. Mom gets home from work.

She walks into the kitchen and sits across from me. "Owen, I thought you would be done by now."

"The printer ran out of ink," I say. "I have to copy the report by

91

hand. It's six pages."

She reads the first page. "I like it," she says. "It's easy to understand. And your printing is neat."

Two hours later, I finish. I glue the report pages to the display board.

I turn the crank on the generator. It lights up every time.

I should be happy. But I'm not.

The project looks bad because the report isn't typed.

17   AT LEAST

WEDNESDAY MORNING. Time to leave for school.

I put a screwdriver, some pliers, and the spare lightbulbs into my backpack.

Mom hugs me. "Owen, good luck," she says. "I think you have a great project."

It's nice of her to say that. But it looks terrible because it's not typed.

Alex knocks on the door. I give him the display board to carry. We walk down the stairs.

"You look wiped out," he says.

"I should. I worked on this until one o'clock in the morning."

"How come you didn't type it?"

"Our printer ran out of ink."

We get to the bottom of the stairs.

"Can I try it?" Alex asks.

He turns the crank, and the light comes on.

"This is great," he says.

MULTI-PURPOSE ROOM. I set up my project.

I wish I could put it in the back. But the spot for Ms. Acosta's classes is in the front.

Brooks also sets up his project. He made a bridge out of popsicle sticks glued together.

It has four jugs of water placed on top of it, thirty-two pounds.

"How did you make it so strong?" I ask.

"I found a video on YouTube. I just did what it said."

He turns the crank on my generator. The light comes on.

"I like how you built it," he says. This thing is solid."

I wish I could smile. But I can't stop thinking about how the report isn't typed.

I walk around and look at the other projects.

There's one with lemons connected to wires that make an electric fan turn.

Somebody else made a project with a tooth that turned black when it got put into Coke for two weeks.

I also see a bogus generator. A light comes on when you push a button and turn a crank.

I know it can't work because it's like the first generator I made.

The person who built it probably hid a battery inside.

My project may look bad because the report isn't typed. But at least I didn't cheat.

SCIENCE. Ms. Acosta comes to the front of the classroom.

"Tomorrow is our day to go to the science fair," she says. "I want to commend all of you who built projects. It's hard to do. And it wasn't required."

I look at Brooks. His bridge holds a lot of weight. I bet he'll get one of the prizes.

LUNCH. The food line is slow. Two guys in front of me start talking. They're the same guys who talked about the van fire.

"Did you go to the science fair?" the first one asks.

"Not yet. Our class is going tomorrow."

"There's a good project. It's an electric generator. You turn a crank, and a light comes on."

"I tried to build a generator last year," the second guy says. "But I couldn't get the light to come on."

"This one works. The faster you turn the crank, the brighter the light gets."

He's talking about my project. I wish the report was typed.

18   REALLY ME

SCIENCE. I take my seat. Nancy and Natalie smile at me.

They usually act like I'm not even there. Something must have happened.

Ms. Acosta comes to the front of the classroom. "When we get to the science fair, be careful when you look at the projects. Don't break anything."

We get to the multi-purpose room. There's a crowd of people at the front.

They're probably looking at the bridge that Brooks made.

But when I get closer, I see they're lining up to turn the crank on my generator.

They're trying to see who can crank the fastest and make the lightbulb burn brightest.

I stand back and watch as they take turns. The light comes on every time.

Even Nancy and Natalie get in line.

PERIOD FOUR. I go back to the science fair. This is the time when we explain our projects to the judges.

I get to the multi-purpose room. My generator still looks good.

But the light doesn't come on

when I turn the crank.

Someone broke it.

I check the wires. None of them are loose. I check the crank and magnets. Those are fine too.

I look at the lightbulb and see the problem. It's scorched inside, burned out.

I open my backpack and take out one of my spare lightbulbs. I connect the wires and turn the crank.

It works.

A lady I don't know watches me. I wonder where she's from.

"Good job," she says.

THIRTY MINUTES LATER. The judges come to me. One of them is the lady who watched me change the lightbulb.

"Owen, how does your project

work?" the first judge asks.

"Electricity is made when magnets spin inside a coil of wire. The spinning magnets cause the electrons in the wire to move. The moving electrons produce an electric current."

"What got you interested in electricity?" the second judge asks.

"I did a report on Thomas Edison. There was a picture in a book of a homemade generator."

"What did you learn from making this project?" the third judge asks. She's the one who watched me change the lightbulb.

"I learned about electricity. I also learned the importance of reading. For the first generator I built, I just copied a video from YouTube without reading anything.

The generator didn't work because I didn't know what I was doing."

"What else did you learn?" she asks.

"When things go bad, you can't give up. When I built this second generator, I thought I had made it wrong because the lightbulb didn't come on. I felt like quitting. But I finally figured out the problem. I was using a lightbulb that was the wrong voltage."

"Anything else?"

"I'm sorry the report isn't typed. Our printer ran out of ink."

"That's okay," the second judge says. "The report is very clear. And your printing is excellent."

"Have you thought about college?" the third judge asks.

"Not really."

"I hope you do," she says. "I'm a professor at Raymond State University. I can tell from your project, and from what you say, that you know what you're talking about. I can see you majoring in electrical engineering. There's a national shortage of people to work in technical fields. The jobs pay a lot of money."

I never thought I would hear anything like this, especially from a professor.

Maybe she's right. Maybe I can go to college someday.

ENGLISH. Class is almost over. The principal's voice comes over the loudspeaker.

"I want to commend all of you who made projects for the science fair," he says. "We had eighty-four entries. The judges said they were outstanding. I will now read the names of the winners."

He reads four names. All of them are eleventh and twelfth graders.

"The final award goes to a tenth grader," the principal says. "The project he built was excellent. I'm pleased to announce the fifth-place winner, Owen Daniels."

Brooks and Esmeralda stand and cheer. Then everybody stands and cheers, even Nancy and Natalie.

Ms. Gulliver writes my name on the board: *Owen Daniels, Fifth Place, Science Fair.*

The bell rings. I look at my name on the board.

It's really me.

19 SMARTER

FRIDAY. English. Ms. Gulliver comes to the front of the classroom.

"I want you to read this article about college scholarships," she says. "You get five minutes. After that, I will call on you."

She passes out the article. I begin reading.

It has a lot of big words. I remember when they were hard for me.

"Owen, could you start?" Ms. Gulliver asks.

I begin reading. "Scholarships in

technical fields are increasing due to shortages in the workforce. Increased financial aid is being made available to students who wish to major in fields such as science, technology, engineering, and mathematics. The Society of Women Engineers awarded several scholarships worth almost five-million dollars last year."

"Very good," Ms. Gulliver says. "Why is the society giving out scholarships?"

"There's a shortage of people to work in technical fields," I say.

"How bad is the problem?"

"I talked to a professor at the science fair. It's a problem all over the country. And the jobs in those fields pay a lot of money."

Ms. Gulliver smiles.

My hours of reading and keeping a word list have paid off.

There's a knock on the door. It's a blue slip for me to see the principal.

I wonder what it's about.

PRINCIPAL'S OFFICE. Dr. Vinson stands and waves me in.

"Owen, I was impressed when I saw your science project yesterday," he says. "The generator was well built. Your report was thorough and clearly written."

I see a framed certificate on his desk. He picks it up.

"I'm proud to give you the Edison Excellence Award," he says. "It's because of your outstanding improvement this year. You have worked very hard."

The certificate is in a polished wooden frame. My name is printed in big letters across the front.

The school secretary comes in and takes our picture as he shakes my hand.

I remember when the school year started. My grades were terrible. I never thought I could get better.

It's been a lot of hard work. And I've read a lot of books.

EVENING. I ride with Uncle Ray in his tow truck.

It's been a slow night. We drive past Edison High School.

"I went to see Ms. Gulliver this afternoon," Uncle Ray says. "She remembered me right away. Then she asked what book I was reading. She's still the same."

"It's funny," I say. "I'll never forget the first day she came to our class. I didn't like her. Then I realized I was lucky to have her."

"She helped both of us," Uncle Ray says. "We were both lucky."

I think about how it was at the beginning of the school year.

I thought I was dumb.

But I worked hard and made myself smarter.

20   DON'T HAVE TO

SATURDAY MORNING. Mike's Market. I go to the front counter and show Mr. Mike my science project.

He turns the crank on the generator and smiles when the light comes on.

He smiles again when he reads the report.

"Owen, can I keep this here for a few days?" he asks.

"What for?"

"I want everybody to see it when they come in to buy something."

I turn the crank again and watch the light come on.

The hard work was worth it.

AFTERNOON. I walk through the crowd at Price Mart.

Mom asked me to paint the kitchen chairs. I have to get some sandpaper.

A man with a paint can walks up to me.

"The printing on this label is too small," he says. "What's the drying time?"

I read the label. It's easy for me now.

"It dries to the touch in one hour," I say. "But you have to wait four hours before you put on a second coat."

I look up. Mom stands behind him.

The man smiles and walks away.

"I remember back in the fall," Mom says to me. "A man asked you for help. You told him you couldn't read the label because you forgot your glasses."

I've changed a lot since then. I feel like a different person now.

HOME. I sit at the kitchen table. My science homework is finished. I get on the laptop and look at School View.

The fifteen-week grades are final now. My science grade went up. I have five B's and one C.

It's the best report card I've ever had.

I look at the new book I got from the library, *Efren Divided*. It will be the thirty-third book I've read this year.

I never thought I would come this far.

I feel good about myself.

I don't have to hide anymore.

RESOURCES

Beaty, William. *Ultra-simple Electric Generator, Wire and Spinning Magnets*, 1996. http://www.amasci.com/amateur/coilgen.html

Cisneros, Ernesto. *Efren Divided*, HarperCollins Publishers, 2020.

Frith, Magaret and John O'Brien illustrator. *Who Was Thomas Alva Edison*? Penguin Workshop, 2005.

General Electric Company, Bray Studios, H. Schroeder. *A Day with Thomas Edison, 1922.* Library of Congress Video. https://www.loc.gov/item/00694187

Tarshis, Lauren. *I Survived Hurricane Katrina*, Scholastic Publishers, 2011.

ACKNOWLEDGMENTS

I would like to express my sincere gratitude to everyone who gave me feedback while I was writing this book.

COFFEE HOUSE WRITERS GROUP: Nicholas Chiazza, Robyn Dolan, Synida Fontes, Helene Hoffmann, J. Bryan Jones, Samantha Hancox-Li, Janelle Hernandez, Julia Kester, Alex Khansa, Brandon Kuys, Phil Levy, John Lowell, Neora Luria, Scott McClelland, Viet Nguyen, Dav Pauli, Jean Pliska, Sarah Skinner, AnneLise Wilhelmsen, and Dennis Wolverton.

SOCIETY OF CHILDREN'S BOOK WRITERS AND ILLUSTRATORS: Lorian Steider Brady, Heather Buchta, Tim Burke,

Rebecca Brewer, Kristine Carter, Melanie Castillo, Ernesto Cisneros, Suzy Creighton, Tacey Derenzy, Jessica Dowsett, Michael Dwyer, Lisa Gold, Chuck Grieb, Trisha de Guzman, Kirsten Hall, Deborah Halverson, Jordan Hamassley, Jamie Hamilton, Christine Henderson, Mark Holtzen, Ryan Harms, Jennie Kendrick, David Larson, Carole Meyer-Rieth, Natascha Morris, Jenny Parsons, Kelly Powers, Linda Ruddy, Christine Rodenbour, Desi St. Amat, Courtney Stevenson, Scott Sussman, Kari Sutherland, Betty Tang, Teri Vitters, Autumn Wetch, Dee White, Annie Young, and Laurie Young.

SOUTHERN CALIFORNIA WRITERS CONFERENCE: Melanie Hooks, Jennie Herrera, Jean Jenkins, Laura

Perkins, Dr. Uwe Stender, Jennifer Silva Redmond, and Claudia Whitsitt.

Thank you, Pam Sheppard, for your advice on creating this series.

Thank you, Laura Perkins, for your careful editing and thoughtful guidance.

Thank you, Betty-Jean, for your patience, your suggestions, your love, and for being my wife.

ABOUT THE AUTHOR

 My dream of becoming a writer started at Whitworth University. I was lucky to have a teacher, Dr. Tammy Reid, who believed in me and encouraged me. After college, I began a career as an educator, teaching reading and English at a middle school in Los Angeles. I later served as a high-school principal. During my many years of working with young people, I observed that every student can succeed. If you can dream it, you can achieve it. Set your sights high, work hard every day, and don't let anything keep you from achieving your dreams.

ADDITIONAL TITLES

NEVER WANTED. Roy Perkins never knew his dad, his mom died in a meth-lab explosion, and his alcoholic uncle beats him. He is sent to live with a caring foster family. But the challenges continue.

TAKEN AWAY. Miles Pruitt has been struggling in high school. When his dad is sent to prison, he quits studying, fails classes, and gets kicked off the basketball team. How will he pick himself up and move forward?

DID YOU ENJOY THIS BOOK? Tell a friend. Write a review on Amazon. Go to www.highinterestpress.com to sign up for information on future titles.

Lightning Source UK Ltd.
Milton Keynes UK
UKHW010629010621
384730UK00001B/116